DINKIN DINGS

AND THE

REVENGE OF THE FISH-MEN

To Mrs Diggle ~ GB

To Catherine – thanks for all the
fish finger sandwiches ~ PW

Check out Dinkin's Bebo page at:
www.bebo.com/dinkindings

STRIPES PUBLISHING
An imprint of Magi Publications
1 The Coda Centre, 189 Munster Road,
London SW6 6AW

A paperback original
First published in Great Britain in 2009

Text copyright © Guy Bass, 2009
Illustrations copyright © Pete Williamson, 2009

ISBN: 978-1-84715-086-8

Printed and bound in Belgium.
10 9 8 7 6 5 4 3 2 1

DINKIN DINGS

AND THE

REVENGE OF THE FISH-MEN

GUY BASS

ILLUSTRATED BY
PETE WILLIAMSON

Stripes

LIFE ACCORDING TO DINKIN DINGS

Dinkin Dings was afraid of everything. And not just actual scary things like being tied to a stampeding elephant or shot into space wearing nothing but a pair of underpants. No, he was afraid of pretty much completely and utterly everything.

There were just three things Dinkin wasn't afraid of:

1. The monster under his bed.
2. The skeleton in his cupboard.
3. The ghost outside his window.

In fact, they were his best friends.

He called them the
Frightening Things.

THE IMPOSTER-BUSTER 500

Chances of Dinkin's dad walking
through the door at any moment: 76%
Chances of Dinkin's dad walking
through the door at any moment
being not-at-all sinister and
terrifying: 0.9%
Chances of Dinkin's dad probably
definitely being an evil robot
(or spy or alien): 88%

"Dinkin, your dad's home!" called Mrs Dings.

"I'll be there in a minute!" said Dinkin. He
peered through the curtains of his bedroom
window as his dad's car pulled up on the
drive.

But was it really him?

Dinkin activated the Imposter-Buster
500 (with patented Reveal-O-Tronic™
technology). He had been assembling the
machine ever since his father had vanished.

Dinkin's mother had been wondering where the vacuum cleaner had gone. And the electric whisk. And eight pairs of her best tights.

This was the fourth time Dinkin's dad had been "away on business" in the last year. Each time he left, he had assured Dinkin that he would be back in a couple of weeks. "It's all just part of my job," his dad would say. But Dinkin knew better. It was far more likely that:

1. Dinkin's dad was a member of an evil organization hell-bent on taking over the world — probably one of the weirder ones like The Secret Spectacle Society, which wanted to make everyone wear glasses. Their meetings took place in a different location each time, so as not to arouse spectacle-related suspicion.

2. Dinkin's dad had been nasally probed by a deeply suspicious race of surprisingly small-headed aliens, and was now under their control. Every now and then he was summoned to the mother ship to gather information about the "stinking flesh-bag earthling scum who stink and are scum".

3. Dinkin's dad was part of Project: "Hey! That Robot Looks Like You!" – a secret government experiment into creating human-like androids for the purposes of warfare and practical jokes. Due to frequent system crashes, Droll Attack Droid (D.A.D.) XP would often have to return to headquarters so the scientists could turn him off and on again.

4. Dinkin's dad had another family in the next street.

"I'm home!" said Dinkin's dad, as he burst through the door. Dinkin crept downstairs, Imposter-Buster 500 in hand.

"Welcome home, Mr Dings... Oh, my! How distinguished!" said Mrs Dings, giving him a peck on the cheek.

What's distinguished? thought Dinkin, panicking. *And what does "distinguished" mean?*

Is it like "extinguished"? As in: "Your life is about to be extinguished, stinking flesh-bag earthling scum!"?

His finger hovered over the Imposter-Buster's "Splatter" button. It was then that he saw it...

A thick strip of hair covering his father's top lip.

A moustache.

"Hello, Dink," said Mr Dings. "How about a hug for your old dad?"

It was exactly as Dinkin had feared. It wasn't his father at all! He'd been replaced! And they hadn't even bothered to make him look right! Was it the government? The aliens? The Secret Spectacle Society? Dinkin didn't have time to decide. He had to act.

"Don't move! Not unless you want to be turned into a cupful of goo!"

"So *that's* where the vacuum cleaner went," tutted Mrs Dings.

"Been working on a new toy, Dinkin?" said his dad. "Let's have a look." He started walking towards Dinkin. There was no choice.

"Stay back!" squealed Dinkin. He set the Imposter-Buster 500 to "Squash" (the least fatal setting – just in case), closed his eyes, and pressed the trigger!

BzzzzzZZZZZzzzzfff—fffsssssss...!

"Same old Dink, always horsing around!" said Mr Dings, ruffling Dinkin's hair. "Right, how about a spot of dinner?"

Dinkin stared at his dad. Where was the squashing? He hadn't even flinched! Not so much as a light flatten!

This day's going to get worse before it gets better, thought Dinkin.

DINNER DANGER

Moustache distraction levels
at 9.684 and rising

Dinkin couldn't believe the Imposter-Buster 500 hadn't worked. What could he have missed? He'd charged the capacitors, primed the plasma-boosters, even emptied the dust-bag! And now, here he was, forced to have dinner with some moustachioed spy/alien slave/robot! How did his mum not notice that he was a fake?

"So, Dink, what have you been up to while I've been away?" asked the dad-double.

Dinkin had actually had a busy couple of weeks. He'd:

1. Rebuilt his Fortress of Ultimate Protection. He had also found a nice big piece of cardboard which made a perfect Door of Indescribable Sturdiness.

2. Created an entirely new language based around clapping, in case he suddenly forgot how to speak.

3. Secretly re-categorized every book in his local library according to scariness.

But he didn't mention any of that to the dad-double – he knew better than to give away important secrets. So instead, he said:

"Nothing at all whatsoever, especially nothing secret or important that you might want to know." Then he took a mouthful of food.

"Well, I was ever so busy," said the dad-double. "Who would have thought you could cram so much team-building into two weeks?"

Dinkin snorted. *Is that the best he can come up with*? *Team-building*? *That is* so *made up*! Dinkin finished the rest of his dinner in silence, working out the necessary modifications to the Imposter-Buster in his head. *Let's see how the dad-double likes the Imposter-Buster 600!*

"So what do you think, Mrs Dings? Should I keep the moustache?" said the dad-double.

"Do you know, as modern and 'today' as it is, I think I prefer you without it," said Mrs Dings. "But I tell you one thing, it's distracted Dinkin long enough for him to eat his dinner without worrying about it."

Dinkin looked at his plate. It was true!

He'd eaten his whole meal without even realizing!

This was probably the first time this had ever happened. Dinkin was terrified of food, and kept a record of his food-related fears (along with all other scariness) in his Daily Diary of Dread and Desperation. The last entry read:

14/03 – 13:38: 'Lunch' – Mrs Hogjaw (code name: The Dinner Lady) tries to give me a baked potato, saying that it will make me "big and strong". I can only conclude that Mrs Hogjaw has developed some sort of secret growth formula and is experimenting on school children. Note to self – to avoid turning into a giant, take packed lunch from now on.

Dinkin stared at his parents, his whole body shaking with fear. It was so obvious – the moustache had just been a decoy! He'd been so obsessed with it that he'd not even considered how scary his dinner could be! What if it was made from some strange, alien substance that had fallen to earth and crawled into the oven? It wouldn't be the first time!

"You see? You said you'd never eat them, but you wolfed them down!" said Mrs Dings.

"Wolfed *what* down? *What did I eat*?" said Dinkin, panicking.

"Well, of course he did!" said Mr Dings. "I mean, who *doesn't* love fish fingers?"

Dinkin went white ... then slightly green ... then back to white again. Suddenly, his dad's moustache didn't matter any more. Suddenly, there was something much, *much* worse to worry about.

"FISH ... F-F-F-F-FINGERS?"

he stuttered in terror.

He leaped out of his chair and rushed to the freezer. He found the fish fingers box and took it out. The box was blue and had a cartoon of an old man on it. He had a white beard and a ridiculously wide, flat hat. Dinkin stared at it in terror.

"SOMETHING FISHY"
FISH FINGERS
OUR SECRET RECIPE
MAKES THESE THE FISHIEST
FISH FINGERS YOU'LL FIND!

"What on earth's the matter, Dinkin? You look like you've seen a ghost," said his mother.

At this moment, a ghost (and not the kind of ghost you can be friends with – even a thoroughly horrid and disgusting ghost, whose sole aim was to haunt Dinkin until his teeth fell out) would have been better than this. This was as bad as it got. This was couldn't-be-worse-even-if-it-tried awful. And there was nothing Dinkin could do about it.

19

The *Fish-Men* were coming.

FISH FINGERS –
A SECRET HISTORY

Number of heads that go missing
in this chapter: 1
Volumes of the Secret History of
the Terrifying: 16
Hours until certain death: 12(ish)

20

Night-time could not come quickly enough for
Dinkin. There was no doubt about it – this was
a job for the *Frightening Things*. Whenever
the world became too scary, whenever there
were dangers that he could not deal with
alone, Dinkin would summon his three best
friends. He took the Ancient Summoning
Parchment and assumed the Ancient
Summoning Position, then he waited for
midnight. Three hours, twelve minutes, forty-
eight seconds and two trips to the toilet later,
he began the Ancient Summoning Chant:

"Frightening Things, Frightening Things,
Creep from the gloom,
Crawl from the shadows and into my room,
Frightening Things, Frightening Things,
Come to my aid,
Save me from danger (and being afraid!)"

Moments later, Herbert the monster emerged from under Dinkin's bed. Well, actually, his smell was the first thing to emerge. It smelled like the sort of mess even a fly wouldn't land on, mixed in with just a touch of honeysuckle.

"I'm hungry," he said. He scratched his tail with a fat claw, green drool dripping from his slack jaws. Just then, the window swung open, and Arthur the ghost flew in.

"It's fr-fr-freezing out there! Look at me, I've turned blue! Well, bluey-white. Have we ever discussed how I'm the only one who has to get here from outside? I could catch my death!"

"You're already dead," said Herbert, picking bits of something not-quite-alive out of his teeth.

"Well, is it any surprise?" he wheezed, then stopped and looked around. "Where's Edgar?"

Suddenly, the cupboard door creaked open and Edgar the skeleton fell out, minus his head. He stumbled around blindly.

"Hello? Dinkin? Are you there? I've had a bit of an accident," said Edgar's head, from inside the cupboard.

"Poor Edgar, always losing his head," laughed Herbert.

I'll just head in there and get it, shall I?" giggled Arthur, flying into the cupboard.

"Oh yes, very amusing. There's nothing like a pun at someone else's expense, now, is there? You two should go into comedy! Stinky and Moany, the Frighteningly Unfunny Things!" said Edgar, grumpily.

"We really don't have time for this..." said Dinkin through gritted teeth. "Can you please hurry up!" Arthur flew out with Edgar's head and popped it on his shoulders.

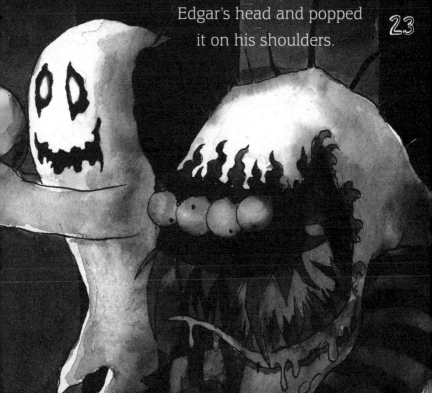

"There you go, Edgar, that should give you a head start!" sniggered Arthur. Herbert let out a belly-laugh, spewing saliva all over the wall.

"No, stop, my sides are splitting!" said Edgar sarcastically, adding, "I mean it – look, I have a loose rib..."

"Excuse me," began Dinkin, desperately trying to remain calm, "but you might want to talk about this stuff *after we've saved me from certain doom*!"

The Frightening Things stopped in their tracks.

"Why? What's happened?" said Edgar. "Is it the family of flesh-eating alien zombies from Beyond Terror who live next door?"

"What? No, of course not, they're *fine*," said Dinkin. "It's something *much* worse.

THE FISH-MEN ARE COMING!"

"*AaAAAA-HHHH!*" screamed Arthur, and he flew into Edgar's mouth. Edgar choked and hacked until, with an almighty sneeze, Arthur shot out of his mouth and into the bedside lamp, making it rock from side to side. Dinkin grabbed the lamp just before it fell (a broken lamp brings at least 756 years' bad luck) and sighed with relief.

Arthur poked his head dizzily out of the top of the lampshade. "Wait, who on earth are the Fish-Men?" he asked.

"I'll tell you, but the truth will *terrify* you," said Dinkin gravely. "Edgar, fetch me ... Volume Six."

"Oh no ... not ... Volume Six! AAaAAAAAAA-HHHH! Wait, which one is Volume Six?" said Arthur.

"The scariest volume of all," s[...]
went across to the bookshelf [...]
with fear, pulled out a large, thick [...]
was one of many. On its cover we[...]

SECRET
HISTORY OF
THE TERRIFYING
Volume Six
(ILLUSTRATED
EDITION)

READ AT YOUR
OWN PERIL!

26

Dinkin had written over sixt[...]
of his Secret History of the [...]
recorded almost every scary th[...]
ever happened to him (or any[...]
could think of), as well as ever[...]
thought he had ever had. The b[...]
such varied topics as GIRLS[...]
ROBOTS, MONKEYS, ROBOT-M[...]
SONGS. No topic was out of bo[...]

took the book from Edgar and
pened it at page one.

FOOD
A list of all
scary, dangerous,
poisonous, evil
and menacing
stuff you can
eat or chew.

turned to the contents page.

ne: Yoghurt – when milk turns evil

o: Rice – maggots or grit?

ree: Crisps – the dandruff of giants

our: Chewing Gum – the sweet that will not die

ve: Soup – half-food, half-drink, all wrong

: Fish – danger from the deep

Dirkin turned to Chapter Six. There it was, the whole truth, spelled out in terrifying black and white. He read it aloud:

FISH FINGERS

The SCARIEST food ever.
FISH FINGERS are, in fact,
the fingers of <u>Fish-Men</u> (see fig. 1).
They were mutated in <u>terrible secret</u>
<u>experiments</u> by some
<u>EVIL MASTERMIND</u> — just to provide
the world with TASTY DINNERS.
The fingerless <u>Fish-Men</u> now live in
the <u>shadows</u>, plotting their <u>revenge</u>
on <u>everyone</u> who eats their fingers.

DO NOT EAT
FISH FINGERS! EVER!

fig. 1

Dinkin closed the book.

"Don't tell me you ate fish fingers..." said Edgar.

"I didn't mean to! I was distracted! My dad had grown a moustache! I thought he was some sort of spy, or evil dad-double!"

"Well, that's all right then – except that we're now DOOMED!" screamed Arthur.

"How many did you eat?" said Herbert, as hungry as he was terrified.

"I ate a whole plateful – I mean, handful! The Fish-Men are going to come after me for sure! And it's not just me – what about Mum and Dad? We're all guilty! They're probably coming for us right now!"

"C-c-c-coming for us? As in *here*?!" screamed Arthur, flying behind Edgar to hide.

"Well, nowhere is safe, obviously. They are killer mutants intent on revenge, after all. Our only chance is to secure the whole area," said Dinkin.

"We're with you, Dinkin! As long as we don't have to do anything, you know, too scary," said Arthur, holding on to Edgar's ribs like they were prison bars. Dinkin rolled up the sleeves of his pyjamas.

"Let's get to work ... it's going to be a long night."

HOW TO STOP
A FISH-MAN
(IN 39 TRAPS OR LESS)

Number of traps set: 39
Time spent setting up anti-Fish-Men
traps: 5 hours 16 minutes
Time before first trap is set off:
56 seconds

By the time the morning sun streamed through the window, everything was ready. Dinkin and the Frightening Things had toiled away for the whole night. Dinkin sat in quite possibly the only safe place in the house, a small patch of floor in the hall.

"Time's up," said Edgar, as he began to fade. "Time for us to disappear. Good luck, Dinkin."

"See you tonight, Dinkin. Hope you don't get turned into fish food," said Herbert. Arthur just waved a ghostly tendril.

Within moments, the Frightening Things had vanished. Dinkin yawned and tried to get comfy. He'd done everything he could. At least his family was protected.

BAM!

"Ow! Ow! My *nose*!" cried his father from upstairs. "What the – why is there a saucepan suspended above our bedroom door? And why did it just *hit me in the face*?"

"It's not a saucepan, it's an Anti-Fish-Men Repelling Hammer™ trap!" said Dinkin, running (very carefully) to the bottom of the stairs. "And it's really better if you don't move!"

"What on earth are you talking about? In fact, what are you even doing out of bed? It's five o'clock in the morning!" said Mr Dings, his foot hovering over the top stair.

"Dad, no! The Anti-Fish-Men Zero-Friction Slip-Wax™ trap!" yelled Dinkin.

But it was too late. As his foot touched

the stair, which was covered in Anti-Fish-Men Zero-Friction Slip-Wax™ (a mix of liquid soap, moisturizer and liberal quantities of olive oil), the floor slid from underneath him. Mr Dings grabbed the banister, but that had been greased too. For a moment he seemed to be doing some sort of strange, slippery dance to steady himself, but it was no use…

SWIP! SLAM! OOF!
FWACK! THUD! SWIP! WUD!
OW! SWIP! "Not the knees!"
WUMP! OOOCH! SWIP!
CRACK! "My face!"
BWAM! "My teeth!"
SLAAAM!! "My moustache!"

Mr Dings tumbled down the stairs, and landed face-first on the bottom step.

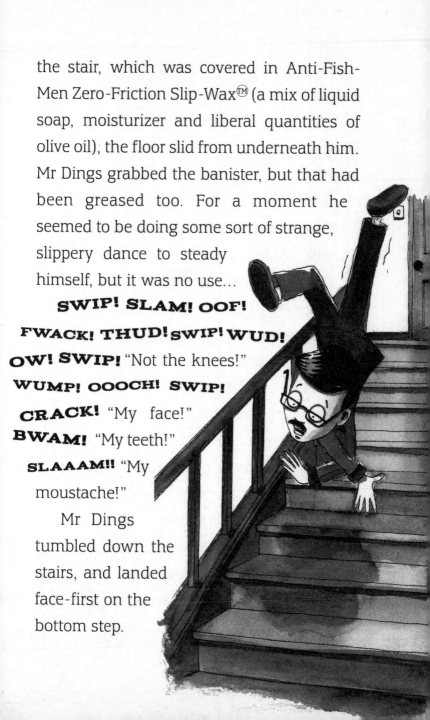

"Dinkin ... would you be a champ and call the hospital?" whimpered Mr Dings.

"What's all this racket – oh, my! Mr Dings!" said Mrs Dings as she came out of the bedroom.

"No! Not the stairs!" cried Dinkin and Mr Dings together. Mrs Dings' foot hovered over the top stair.

"Don't move!" cried Dinkin. "You're ruining everything! I was up all night with the Frightening Things laying anti-Fish-Men traps! The whole house is booby-trapped!"

Dinkin's mother froze.

"Did you say ... *booby-trapped*?" she said, her eyes wide with rage. "What have I told you about booby-trapping the house?!"

"You said I absolutely, definitely, categorically shouldn't do it ... but that was before we knew about the Fish-Men! It's not my fault – it's the evil mastermind who mutated them in the first place!" cried Dinkin.

"Fish-Men?" said Mrs Dings.

"The fingerless Fish-Men, who were mutated by the evil mastermind to be part fish, part man so that he could chop off their fingers and feed them to us, and who are now out for revenge on all those who ate their fingers!" cried Dinkin, in a single, desperate breath.

"That seems like an awful lot of work just to get some fish fingers," said Mr Dings as he checked to see whether he still had all his teeth. "Still, you never know – they are *disturbingly* tasty..." he smirked.

"*Please* don't encourage him, Mr Dings..." said Mrs Dings through gritted teeth, her eyes darting around for signs of booby-trappery. "Dinkin, listen to me. There are no Fish-Men. There are fish, and there are men. And women, and children, and dogs, and hamsters. But no Fish-Men! Now dismantle these traps and get ready for school!"

"School? I can't go to school! Our only chance is to hide ourselves in here and hope there are enough traps! And if that doesn't work, we'll have to use the tunnel..." said Dinkin.

"Dinkin, we're not staying here and you're not having another day off sch—. Wait, did you say tunnel?" said his mother.

"Well, technically it's not an actual tunnel, because it only goes from the garden to a very-tiny-bit-further-down-the-garden, but once I've perfected my Semi-Atomic Magna-Mole Hyperborizer Drill™ we'll be able to dig our way to Australia! Well, OK, not Australia, because the whole place is upside down, and you don't need me to tell you how terrifying *that* sounds... But it's still a better plan than sending me to school!"

"Dinkin Danger Dings, I have heard quite enough silliness for one day. Now get your school uniform on before—" began Mrs Dings, taking a step back into Dinkin's Anti-Fish-Men

Grab 'n' Lift Ankle-Snagger™ trap. She was immediately lifted foot-first into the air.

"AaaAAaa—AHHHaH!" she screamed, dangling upside down like meat in a butcher's shop.

"Hang on, darling! I'm coming," said Mr Dings, scrambling to his feet. He tried desperately to climb the stairs, but no matter how fast he ran or how carefully he crawled, he always ended up at the bottom.

"**GET ME DOWN!**" shrieked Mrs Dings.

"I'll get something to clean up all this gloop – wait there," continued Mr Dings, hurrying into the kitchen.

"Watch out for the Anti-Fish-Men Freakishly Forceful Face-Flattener™ tra— " began Dinkin.

BLANG!

"Never mind."

TRIP AHOY!

Chances of Dinkin being sent
to school: 81%
Chances of Dinkin waking up
and it all being a dream: 0.3%
Chances of things turning out
worse than expected: 98.7%

Two hours, thirty-nine minutes, and nineteen traps later, Dinkin was in his school uniform.

"You can't send me! They're out there! They won't be happy until we've all paid for eating their fingers!"

"You'll d-d-do what you're t-t-told," said Mrs Dings, still sparking from the Anti-Fish-Men Hectic All-Electrical™ trap. As the bus trundled down the road, she hurried Dinkin up the drive and waved it down. The bus driver screeched to a halt at the sight of Mrs Dings holding Dinkin with one hand and

a mysterious black slime fr[...]
[...]eft over from the Anti-Fis[...]
[...] Gunk 'Em™ trap) with the ot[...]
[...]ease take this boy to school, an[...]
[...] gets to his classroom," she sai[...]
[...]ver, picking splinters out of h[...]
[...]the Anti-Fish-Men Shard 'n[...]
[...]uard™ trap). "And *please*, Din[...]
[...]onsense about Fish-Men!"

Of course, all of the other children on the bus heard Dinkin's mum say "Fish-Men", and immediately began chanting it. By the time he got to school, Dinkin had heard "Fish-Men" 418 times. As he hurried into the classroom, his nerves were more shredded than ever.

And school was bad enough as it was. As anyone who has ever been to school will tell you, it's a fairly unpleasant experience, but when you're scared of everything, it really is *much* worse. Dinkin's usual day was crammed with scariness. Apart from the day to day problems of teachers, lessons, bullies and girls, Dinkin had a thousand other terrible things to contend with. His top five Surprisingly Scary School Stresses were:

1. The school bell — Dinkin felt the need to "duck and cover" under his desk every time it went off.

2. Strip lights — overexposure can

lead to rampant werewolf-ism.

3. "School smell" – the reason all schools smell the same is because of the mind-control dust they pump through the air vents. Dinkin held his breath a lot during the school day.

4. That dream where you're at school and you realize that somehow, you're not wearing any clothes.

5. Waking up and realizing it's not a dream at all (and everyone's staring).

But today, Dinkin wasn't really worried about school. He wasn't worried about anything except Fish-Men.

"Right then class, listen carefully," said Ms Feebleback. "As soon as I've finished the register we're getting on the coach. I hope you've all got your permission slips."

Coach? *Permission slips*? thought Dinkin. *The only reason I'd need a permission slip is if I was going on a ...*

SCHOOL TRIP!

Dinkin frantically reached for his Daily Diary of Dread and Desperation. He flicked to today's date. It said:

SCHOOL TRIP!
DANGER LEVEL: 11/10
DO NOT RETURN
PERMISSION SLIP!
AT ALL!

Dinkin had forgotten all about it! School trips terrified Dinkin more than school! *Don't panic!* he thought, even though telling himself not to panic always made him panic in the end. He took a few deep breaths and assessed the situation. Three things were clear:

1. He hadn't given his mother the permission slip to sign.

2. Without a permission slip, there would be no school trip.

3. He was saved!

"I'm saved!" cried Dinkin very loudly.

"Is there a problem, Dinkin?" said Ms Feebleback, looming over him. Dinkin tried not to smile.

"Sorry, Ms Feebleback, I haven't got my permission slip. I'd love to come on what I'm sure will be a fascinating and educational outing, but my mum said no," said Dinkin.

"Did she now?" said Ms Feebleback. "May I see your bag, please?" Dinkin handed her his satchel with a look of suspicion. She reached inside it and nimbly peeled back a secret pocket sewn into the lining.

How long has that been there? Will I never escape Mum's scarily secret sewing? thought Dinkin.

"The thing is, your *mother* telephoned me last week. She told me that she'd found the permission slip and that she'd hidden it in your bag for me," said Ms Feebleback, pulling it out with a victorious sniff. "In fact, she said a nice school trip would be good for you. Wasn't that kind of her?"

"B-b-b-but..." began Dinkin. He was panicking far too much to think of anything creative to say, so he plumped for one of his forty-six stock reasons for not doing stuff. "Miss, I'm not well! I have a cold! I mean, a cough! A dysfunction of the under-guts! Seeping bottom-pops! Volcanic mucus!"

"Well, that's strange," began Ms Feebleback, "because look what it says on the *other* side of the slip..."

P.S. Dinkin is not in the least bit ill, even if he says he is.

And he definitely doesn't have volcanic mucus.

Yours sincerely,
Mrs Dings

"So you see, there's no escape," said Ms Feebleback with a smug grin. "Now get your coat – it's time to go..."

Dinkin had officially run out of ideas. He could have pretended to faint again, but last time he did that he ended up being poked and prodded by Nurse Belch for three hours, which was even worse than a school trip. There was nothing else for it but to accept his fate.

At least now he didn't feel so bad about all those traps his mum and dad had to deal with...

THE BIT BEFORE THE BIT WHERE EVERYTHING GOES REALLY WRONG

Chances of everything going really wrong in a bit: 99.2%

On the coach, Dinkin sat next to Boris Wack, the biggest boy in class. Boris was well-known for punching everything that he didn't understand, so Dinkin thought he'd be good to have around if any Fish-Men showed up.

"You want me to give you a dead leg?" said Boris, clenching an enormous fist.

"N-n-n-no thanks. I'm, uh, I'm allergic to dead legs," said Dinkin. Boris looked a bit confused. That was the good thing about Boris. He was thicker than school custard, so it was usually easy to baffle him.

Dinkin leaned forward. "Uh, Miss, are we nearly there yet?" But Ms Feebleback was busy talking to the coach driver, Mr Lagfoot. He quickly asked another nine times.

"As I told you five minutes ago, it'll be another five minutes!" said Ms Feebleback, adding, "I knew you'd be excited once we got under way."

Dinkin sighed. He'd never been excited about a school trip, and with good reason. Every year they were more terrifying than the last. So far Dinkin had endured:

TRIP 1: The Paper Factory –
PAPER-CUT HAZARD: 6.9.9.2
KiloScares (as measured on Dinkin's
patented Threat-O-Meter™)

TRIP 2: The Cheese Factory –
DAIRY DROWNING DANGER: 7.8.9.1
KiloScares

TRIP 3: The Biscuit Factory –
C.C.C.T. ("CHRONIC CRUMB
CONTAMINATION" THREAT): 9.9.9.4
KiloScares

This one's bound to be just as bad, thought Dinkin. It was then that it occurred to him – he hadn't even asked where they were going. Still, at least he should be safe from—

"Here we are children, all safe and sound," said Ms Feebleback, as the coach pulled into the car park. "What an exciting day we have ahead ... at the 'Something Fishy' fish finger factory!"

EVIL MASTERMINDS AND HOW TO SPOT THEM

Number of evil masterminds: 1
Number of ridiculously wide,
flat hats: 1
Number of big, white beards: 1

Dinkin stared in horror at the sign by the entrance:

YOU ARE NOW ENTERING THE
"SOMETHING FISHY"
FISH FINGER FACTORY.
THERE'S SOMETHING REALLY
FISHY GOING ON IN HERE!

It can't be! thought Dinkin. *Why didn't I ask where we were going? Why didn't I pretend to faint? Even Nurse Belch's sandpaper hands would be better than this!*

"Come on, Dinkin, you've made it this far. Don't you want to see how fish fingers are made?" said Ms Feebleback.

"AaaaaAA-AAAAH!" screamed Dinkin. He was about to make a break for it, when Ms Feebleback blocked his path.

"Don't even think about running, Dinkin Dings – I'm in no mood for a chase."

"Please!" screamed Dinkin, gripped with fear. "You can't send me in there! The horror, the horror!"

"Dinkin, every day you remind me that I don't get paid enough to do this job," she said, shooing him off the coach. "See you in a few hours, Mr Lagfoot – keep an eye out for any escaping children."

"Will do!" said Mr Lagfoot.

Ms Feebleback steered a protesting Dinkin into the factory, closely followed by the rest of 5D. They filed into a huge, grey room, full of conveyor belts and great, grinding machines. The whole building hummed and whirred as if it was alive. Above them was a long metal gantry, running all the way around the room and leading to dozens of (probably secret) rooms.

"It stinks of fish!" said Misty Spittle, sending a fine spray of saliva into the air. If anyone was going to notice smells, it was Misty. She had the biggest nose in the whole school. It was so terrifyingly large that Dinkin was sure it contained a black hole.

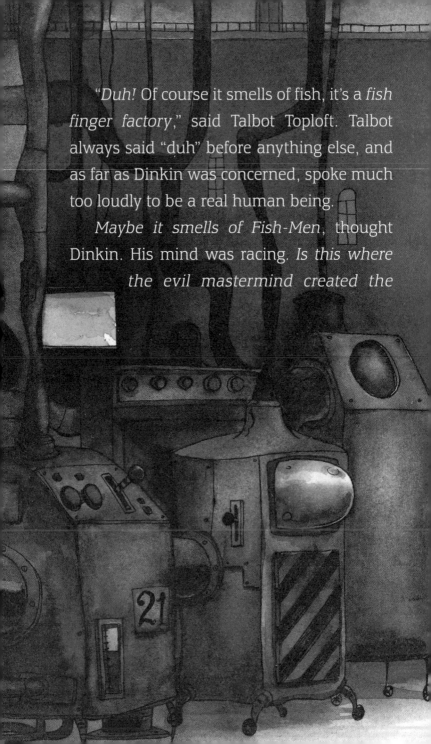

"*Duh!* Of course it smells of fish, it's a *fish finger factory*," said Talbot Toploft. Talbot always said "duh" before anything else, and as far as Dinkin was concerned, spoke much too loudly to be a real human being.

Maybe it smells of Fish-Men, thought Dinkin. His mind was racing. *Is this where the evil mastermind created the hideous mutant Fish-Men? What if the Fish-Men know I'm here? I can feel their beady eyes on me! They think I love fish fingers – now they're going to think they're all I eat! Oh, this day can't get any worse!*

BAAAAAAAAARRRRRRRRRRP!!!

"AAa-A-aAH!" screamed Dinkin. "It's the foghorn of Doom! The nineteenth sign of the end of the world! Duck and cover!"

Dinkin scurried between Boris Wack's tree-trunk-thick legs. "Why is no one ducking and covering?" he cried.

"Oh, *do* behave yourself, Dinkin," sighed Ms Feebleback, dragging him to his feet. "That just means it's time for the presentation."

"Here comes Pip Ahoy! Yay!" came a cry. From out of nowhere, an unusually short man appeared. He was wearing a blue-and-white striped T-shirt and a small white hat. He looked like a cross between a sailor and an annoying children's TV presenter.

"Hi kids! I'm Pip Ahoy, your guide to the world of 'Something Fishy' fish fingers! Yay! Who here loves fish fingers?"

"No, I hate them! I didn't even mean to eat them! Down with evil masterminds!" shouted Dinkin, but he was drowned out by the happy cheers of twenty-two hungry children.

"Yeah, of course you love fish fingers! Yay! And I bet you love 'Something Fishy' fish fingers the best, don't you, kids? That's because only 'Something Fishy' fish fingers are made to a super-secret recipe!" continued Pip Ahoy.

"Ms Feebleback, I, um, need to go to the toilet!" pleaded Dinkin, desperate to find an escape route. But Ms Feebleback was too busy cheering to listen.

"And there's only one person in the world who knows the secret of the super-secret recipe – the mastermind behind 'Something Fishy' fish fingers!" said Pip Ahoy.

Dinkin froze. *Did he just say ... mastermind?*

"And you know who that is, don't you, kids?" said Pip Ahoy.

"Yeah!" said twenty-two children.

"You do? Who? Who?" cried Dinkin, shaking Misty Spittle by the shoulders. A spray of cheek-warmed saliva showered the nearby children as Misty tried to speak through the shaking.

"Ad-Ad-Admiral Anchor," she stammered.

"That's right, kids!" said Pip Ahoy. "The genius behind 'Something Fishy' fish fingers ... is Admiral Anchor! Yay!"

A door opened out on to the high gantry above. Everyone looked up. From the darkness came an old man, as tall as a tree and with teeth like glasses of milk. He had a white beard and a ridiculously wide, flat hat. He looked identical to the cartoon on the fish finger packet!

"Avast ye, land lubbers! Hoist the mizzen-mast! Splice the mainbrace! Swab the poop deck and make ready!" said Admiral Anchor. For some reason, everyone cheered. "Well shiver me timbers, it's a pleasure to see you all, here at my 'Something Fishy' fish finger factory!" Admiral Anchor straightened his ridiculous hat and made his way down the gantry stairs.

"This is where we make the fishiest fish fingers on the seven seas – the secret's in the 'Something Fishy' super-secret recipe!"

Every now and again, Dinkin would have one of those days that got worse with every minute. This was definitely one of those days. He'd come face to face with the evil mastermind that created the Fish-Men! He was so close that Dinkin could actually smell his evilness! Dinkin froze with terror. Only his eyes still seemed to work, and they searched around for a possible escape route.

Admiral Anchor turned to Talbot Toploft. "And what's your name, young scallywag?"

"*Duh*, my name's Talbot Toploft," said Talbot.

"A fine, seafaring name! Welcome aboard!" bellowed Admiral Anchor. "And what about you, young man?"

"My name's Boris, Your Majesty! Aye aye, Your Majesty!" said Boris, who always got confused around figures of authority.

"A marvellous name! You'll make a fine addition to my crew! And what about you, sonny?" he said to Dinkin.

"Evil mastermind!" said Dinkin accidentally. Admiral Anchor peered at Dinkin, his eye twitching slightly. "I mean, Dinkin Dings..." whispered Dinkin.

"Excellent! I must say, I've never seen such a proud bunch of sailors in all my days! I bet you could all serve as my crew aboard the HMS *Fishbone*!" said Admiral Anchor.

"But if you're going to crew my vessel, you'll need to get your strength up! Pip, these children look hungry. What say we feed them up with 'Something Fishy'?"

"Oh, no..." whimpered Dinkin.

"Aye aye, Admiral! Follow me, everyone! Yay!" cried Pip Ahoy.

A FEAST OF
FISH FINGERS

Approximate fish fingers total: 428
Probability of Dinkin jumping on
to a table: 77.4%
Number of times Talbot Toploft
says "Dinkin duh!": 8

Pip Ahoy skipped across the room to two large, metal doors. The children followed without question, and Ms Feebleback shepherded Dinkin along at the back. The wave of children parted as Admiral Anchor approached the doors. With an almost super-human push, he swung them open.

"Dig in, me hearties!" he said.

The room was huge and full of brightly-coloured balloons. Each one had a picture of Admiral Anchor's face on it. In the centre of the room was a large table. On it were plates

upon plates of steaming hot "Something Fishy" fish fingers.

"No... What have you done?" cried Dinkin, his eyes darting from one finger-filled plate to another.

"Fish fingers! Yay!" squealed Pip Ahoy.

"Help yourselves! There's plenty for everyone!" said Admiral Anchor. The children sat down, and everyone started scoffing the fish fingers as if they hadn't eaten in days. Then Admiral Anchor winked at Dinkin and said, "Just don't ask what the super-secret recipe is!"

…Which was just enough to push Dinkin over the edge. He leaped on to the table and started grabbing fish fingers out of people's hands!

"NO! Everyone, stop! You don't know what you're eating! These aren't fish fingers! I mean, they *are,* but they're not! You have to believe me – the Fish-Men will get you! They'll get us all! No one is safe!"

"Dinkin Dings, come down from there!" shrieked Ms Feebleback.

"But it's true! They're the fingers of *Fish-Men!* Hideous, mutated Fish-Men who want revenge on all those who eat their fingers! And it's all his fault!" cried Dinkin, pointing at Admiral Anchor with a fish finger.

"Who? Me?" said Pip Ahoy, who was standing next to Admiral Anchor.

"No, *him!* The evil mastermind! Admiral Anchor! He's the one who's been mutating the Fish-Men! He's the one who's been turning their fingers into food, and now they want revenge! They want to turn us into food – fish food!"

There was silence. Actual no-noise-at-all silence. It was so quiet that you could hear the air passing through Misty Spittle's vast nostrils. Everyone in the room stared at Dinkin for what seemed like for ever. Ms Feebleback shook her head.

"It's true," squeaked Dinkin.

"Of *course* it's true, Dinkin. It's all true!" said Ms Feebleback, her face going red. "Just like it's true that the sun is going to explode, or blackbirds are vampire bats in disguise, or your neighbour is an alien space zombie! I am sick and tired of your silly stories, Dinkin Dings! Now, get off the table at once!"

"But—" began Dinkin.

"NOW!" screeched Ms Feebleback.

By the time Dinkin had climbed down from the table, everyone was laughing at him (except for Talbot Toploft, who kept saying "Dinkin duh!" over and over). Dinkin had never felt so small in all his life. With the other children still laughing, Ms Feebleback dragged him out of the factory and back on to the coach. "Now, you'll stay here and think about what you've done," she said, sitting Dinkin down on the back seat. "Keep an eye on him for me, Mr Lagfoot."

"Leave him with me, right? Right!" said Mr Lagfoot.

Ms Feebleback stormed off the coach and headed back towards the factory. Dinkin looked around and breathed a very small sigh of relief. The further away he was from Admiral Anchor and the fish finger factory, the better. He would have been happy to stay on the coach for the rest of the day.

Unfortunately, that wasn't going to be an option...

THE UNBEARABLE TIGHTNESS OF BLADDER

Danger of Fish-Men attack: 44.8%
Danger of evil mastermind attack: 65.3%
Danger of exploding: 89.9%

Three hours and forthy-one minutes later, Dinkin needed the toilet more than he had ever needed the toilet before. He'd always been frightened of "holding it in" because he thought it turned him into a ticking wee-bomb, but the idea of leaving the coach was even more terrifying. By the time he decided that exploding was probably the more permanent of the two problems, he could hardly move. He shuffled down the coach like he was carrying a ping-pong ball between his knees, and found Mr Lagfoot reading the newspaper.

"Need ... the ... toilet," said Dinkin, barely able to speak.

"Toilet, right? Right!" said Mr Lagfoot, who said "right" more than any human being should. "I went when we got here. In through that side door, right? Right! Then turn right and then left, right? Then another left and you're there, right? Right, left, left, right? Right!"

"Right...?" squeaked Dinkin, doubled over in pain.

"Right! Go on, hurry up – and don't forget to come straight back, right? Right!"

Dinkin's eyes widened with fear. Go back in there *on his own*? He winced with bladder-bursting pain and hobbled off the coach.

The car park seemed like a tarmac ocean of terrifying possibilities, but anything was better than exploding. It seemed to take for ever to cross, and all the while Dinkin expected an army of Fish-Men to jump out and grab him.

At least if I explode, I might take a couple of them with me, he thought.

At last Dinkin reached the side door of the factory and nervously, painfully opened it. He stepped inside into a drab, grey corridor.

"Right ... left ... left ... right. No wait ... right ... left ... right, right?" he said to himself, already confused. He shuffled further down the corridor, looking around desperately for any signs of a) Fish-Men, b) evil masterminds and c) a toilet. Two rights, three lefts (or maybe four) and one accidental double-back later, he found himself in front of a large door, upon which was a scary-looking sign.

SECRET SECTOR OMEGA 3
TOP LEVEL CLEARANCE ONLY
(SUPER-SECRET RECIPE SECRETS INSIDE!)

This must be where Admiral Anchor does all his mutating! thought Dinkin, panicking. This was much closer than he ever wanted to be to the super-secret Fish-Men mutation chambers! It was too terrifying for his bladder to take – even the slightest scare could make him explode outright! He doubled back as fast as he could (which wasn't very fast) and...

DWUFF!

...ran straight into Pip Ahoy!

"AAA-AH!" screamed Dinkin.

It took every last ounce of his strength not to explode!

"Don't worry, it's me – Pip Ahoy! Yay!" said Pip in a horribly cheerful voice.

"Wasn't ... doing ... anything!" said Dinkin, straining to keep himself together. "Looking ... for ... the ... toilet!"

"Well, you won't find it in super-secret Secret Sector Omega 3, silly!" giggled Pip. "Not that I'd know – I've never been in there. Nobody's allowed in there except the Admiral himself – that's where he does all his super-secret stuff ... like working on his super-secret recipe! Yay!"

"Um ... toilet ... please..." squeaked Dinkin, more desperate than ever to get away.

"What? Oh, yes! Toilet! Follow me. Yay!" said Pip Ahoy, and led Dinkin to the nearest lavatory. Of course, Dinkin thought public toilets were unbearably frightening, but today there was no way he could avoid it. He just went. The relief was so tremendous it was almost scary. But as soon as he had finished, Fish-Men-related panic set in again.

"How come you're still here, anyway?" said Pip Ahoy as Dinkin hurried out of the toilet. He was looking out of the window into the car park. "I mean, isn't that your coach leaving?"

"WHAT?" shrieked Dinkin. He rushed to the window. The coach! It was MOVING! Dinkin started running as fast as he could down the corridor! He quickly realized that he probably should have asked Pip Ahoy for directions – he still had no idea where he was. By the time he had turned left, right, left, left (which was a dead end), right, left, right and finally found the door to the outside, the coach was almost out of the gates.

"Wait! Come back! I'm still here! Boy overboard!" he cried. He raced after the coach as fast as he could, calling out the names of every classmate he could remember. He jumped up and down and waved his arms, but it was no use. The coach drove off down the road and disappeared. Dinkin kept running until he reached the gates, then sank to his knees, exhausted. "I'm still here..." he panted again.

They were gone.

He was alone.

Dinkin looked around. Behind him, the towering fish finger factory cast a terrifying shadow. He was lost, and miles from home. Then, because terror comes in pairs, a dark shadow loomed over him.

"Looks like the ship sailed without the full crew..."

Dinkin turned around and

looked up. The white beard and ridiculously wide, flat hat were unmistakable.

It was Admiral Anchor.

"**AAA-AAA-AAHH!**" screamed Dinkin, and ran!

"What? No, it's OK! Come back!" shouted Admiral Anchor, grabbing Dinkin by the sleeve of his jumper. Dinkin shrieked again, but Admiral Anchor held on tight. Fortunately, Dinkin was wearing his Getaway Jumper™ Mark IV. He tugged at a small tab just below his shoulder, and the sleeve came off! He darted into the sea of parked cars, leaving Admiral Anchor with a handful of sleeve and an increasingly concerned look on his face.

"Come back! This is a car park, not a playground! You could get hurt!" yelled the admiral.

That's just the sort of thing an evil mastermind masquerading as a child-friendly maker of fish products would say, thought a panicked Dinkin. He hid behind a car and held his breath. After an unbearably long eighteen seconds, Dinkin ducked under the car to see if he could spot any feet. Nothing! He must have gone the other way, which meant Dinkin had a clear run to the road! He took a deep breath, and ran.

"Stop!" yelled Admiral Anchor. Dinkin had been spotted! He looked back to see Admiral Anchor spring into action! Dinkin ran and screamed until he could no longer feel either his legs or his face, but Admiral Anchor just kept coming. He was almost at the open gates when he took one last terrified look back.

Dinkin had run face-first into the "You are now entering the 'Something Fishy' fish finger factory" sign. He bounced off and fell limply to the floor, his head spinning. The last thing he saw before he passed out was Admiral Anchor looming over him.

NOT-SO-ADMIRAL SIMON

Important revelation count: 11½
Actual Admiral count: 0
Scary things Dinkin has done
for no reason at all count: 5

When Dinkin woke up, he was still lying on the tarmac of the "Something Fishy" fish finger factory car park. Admiral Anchor was patting his hand repeatedly.

"Oh, thank goodness! Are you all right?" said Admiral Anchor.

"AAAAA—"

"*Please* don't scream!" begged Admiral Anchor, holding his temples. "I get terrible migraines. How are you feeling?" Dinkin decided not to answer, in case he gave anything important away. "Dinkin – it is Dinkin, isn't it? Well, the thing is, Dinkin, you've had a bump on the head. And your coach seems to have left without you. Can you tell me where you live so I can give you a lift home?"

"What? No!" begged Dinkin, panicking. "I can't be seen with you! The Fish-Men are already after me! If they see me with the evil mastermind they'll want even *more* revenge!"

"Dinkin, I'm really *not* an evil—" began Admiral Anchor.

"I didn't mean to eat their fingers!" cried Dinkin. "It was a mistake! I didn't know what I was doing! Fish-Men, spare me!" Admiral Anchor rubbed his eyes and sighed a long, exhausted sigh.

"Dinkin, we seem to have got off on the wrong foot. I'm not sure what all this Fish-Men business is, but the fact is I can't possibly be an evil mastermind ... because I'm *not* Admiral Anchor. I'm not even a real admiral. Look..." Admiral Anchor reached up slowly and took off his ridiculously wide, flat hat ... and with it came the beard! They were *attached* – the beard was a fake!

"Wh-what's going on?" said Dinkin, staring helplessly at the hat-beard.

"My name is Simon, and I'm an *actor*," he replied with a smile.

Could it be a trick? Dinkin thought, edging backwards along the ground. *I was tricked by facial hair yesterday!*

"The fact is, there *is* no Admiral Anchor. He's just a character made up by the people at 'Something Fishy' to help sell fish fingers. I've been playing the Admiral for a couple of months now – it's the only thing that's ever paid me any real money," sighed Not-so-Admiral Simon. "But I'd give anything to play Hamlet..."

"But ... your super-secret recipe ... Secret Sector Omega 3 ... the Fish-Men..." said Dinkin, his mind flooded with terrifying doubts.

"Oh, Dinkin, there are no Fish-Men. Those fish fingers are just plain old battered cod. And all that Secret Sector Omega 3 stuff is just what they put on there for the school trips. Oh, and you want to know what the super-secret recipe is? Salt. Lots and *lots* of salt."

Not-so-Admiral Simon held out his hat-beard. Dinkin reached out like a nervous squirrel and stroked the beard hair. It didn't feel like hair at all – it felt like a fancy dress wig. Dinkin suddenly felt rather strange. If Admiral Anchor *wasn't* an evil mastermind (or even a real admiral), then maybe, just maybe, fish fingers weren't actually fingers. Maybe they were just called fish fingers ... which would mean there weren't any Fish-Men. And that would mean he had...

1. Booby-trapped the whole house.

2. Trampled an entire table's worth of fish fingers.

3. Been laughed at by the whole of class 5D.

4. Missed the coach home.

5. Run away from an actor and knocked himself out.

...for no reason at all. Dinkin felt the frankly scary bump on his head, and started to feel a bit silly.

"I think I need to go home," he said, realizing that he had absolutely no idea where he was. Sixteen brand new things immediately terrified him, from the possibility that he would be run over, to an attack by cyber-starlings.

"No problem, I'll give you a lift ... but no more screaming. I'm really not a fan of the screaming," said Simon the actor, helping Dinkin to his feet.

Dinkin found out all about Simon the actor on the way home. He was 45, a Taurus, and scared of bats, bees and spiders, but only hairy ones. By the time they walked up the drive to the door, Dinkin had all but forgotten about the Fish-Men.

"I bet your mum and dad will be glad to see you," said Simon, reaching for the doorbell. Suddenly, Dinkin remembered the booby traps.

"No, don't!" he cried.

DING DONG!

LOST AND FOUND

Number of traps located/set off: 32
Number of traps remaining: 7

Mrs Dings opened the door to find a man dressed in an admiral's uniform lying flat on his back. Next to him lay a ridiculously wide hat and a fake white beard ... and on the other side of him stood Dinkin.

"Dinkin! What happened?"

"Anti-Fish-Men Doorbell Decimator™ trap," said Dinkin, pointing at the spring-loaded bag of garden tools that had just swung into Simon's face.

"H-hello ... you must be Mrs Dings..." groaned Simon.

"Oh dear, are you all right?" said Mrs Dings, helping Simon into the house. Two cups of tea and a long explanation later, things had started to make a sort of sense.

"Thank you so much for bringing Dinkin home, Simon," said Mr Dings, offering him a ginger nut. "He's a live wire, isn't he? We've tried to tell him how things are, but in the end he just believes what he wants."

"No harm done," said Simon, rubbing his swollen nose. "Well, I'd better be off." He picked up his hat and beard, and then paused for a moment. He walked over to Dinkin, and placed the hat-beard on Dinkin's head.

"Here, you keep it. I'm thinking of a change of direction anyway," he said.

"Is it disinfected?" said Dinkin, quickly taking off the beard. Simon just laughed.

"You worry too much," he said, ruffling Dinkin's hair. And with that, he shook hands with Mr and Mrs Dings and left.

"He didn't answer the question," murmured Dinkin, suspiciously.

"Of course it's clean! Actors are always clean. Now then, how about you make sure there are no traps left to dismantle, and I'll cook you some nice dinner. OK?" said Dinkin's mother.

"How many have you found?" said Dinkin, nervously.

"Thirty-one so far," said Mrs Dings.

SPWONG!

"OW! My backside!" cried Mr Dings, accidentally activating the Anti-Fish-Men All-Out Armchair Assault™ trap.

"Make that thirty-two…" sighed Mrs Dings. "Now, what do you fancy for dinner?"

Dinkin looked at his hat-beard and said, "Fish fingers, please."

PUTTING ON THE HAT-BEARD

Traps dismantled: 7
Fish fingers eaten: 4
Hat-beards worn: 1

Dinkin had just finished dismantling the Anti-Fish-Men Flatten-U-Flat™ trap when his mum called him for dinner. This time, he tucked into his fish fingers like he hadn't eaten in days.

"There are more if you want them," said Mrs Dings.

"Can we have them tomorrow?" said Dinkin, shovelling in another surprisingly unscary mouthful.

"Why not?" she said, then started to chuckle. "You see, Dinkin? Sometimes things aren't scary at all. In fact sometimes, they're really rather normal."

"I suppose," said Dinkin, and even though it sounded like a ridiculous statement at the time, it was all he thought about for the rest of the evening. It meant that he entirely forgot to be scared about:

1. The dangers of lightning-conducting vegetables (notably broccoli and asparagus) as he watched a TV programme about cooking outside.

2. Melting/blowing up/bursting into flames/shrivelling up like a raisin as he sat next to the electric fire.

3. Having his feet snipped off by Stair-crabs as he made his way up to bed.

As he put on his pyjamas, Dinkin decided that being scared of everything was actually pretty tiring. Maybe it was time to stop being scared altogether. Life would be so much simpler. He was about to put his hat-beard into the Quarantizer (made from a shoebox, six and-a-half rolls of clingfilm and a jelly mould) for a molecular-level clean, but then, quite without thinking, he put it on his head. He looked at himself in the mirror. Obviously, as he looked like a child with a ridiculously wide, flat hat and white beard, it was quite a scary sight, but there was also something strangely comforting about it.

"Tomorrow I'm not going to be scared of anything," he said. He got into bed without checking for sub-atomic pillow-pirates, and didn't even think about summoning the Frightening Things. He just stroked his beard until he fell asleep.

THEY CAME FROM BEYOND THE PLUGHOLE

Chances of Dinkin needing to go to the toilet in the night: 99.4%
Chances of Dinkin's toothbrush flying across the bathroom: 93.2%
Chances of everything turning out to be really rather normal: 0.1%

Dinkin didn't wake up until 02:52, which was the longest he had slept without waking up in two years, six months and nine days. He got up to go to the toilet, and didn't bother to turn on the light. He didn't even bother to take his Nocturnator™, a sort of torch/water-pistol combination for tackling dangers after dark. He did have a bit of a shock when he saw himself in the bathroom mirror, but in the end it just made him giggle. It was as if nothing could frighten him...

That is, until he saw his toothbrush start to shake in its cup. Next, the shampoo began shuddering on the edge of the bath. Within seconds everything that was not tied down was shaking like there was an earthquake!

"M-M-Mum?" whimpered Dinkin, quaking with fear. As he backed towards the door, the plughole began to open! Within seconds it was as big as a manhole cover!

Voooosh! Dinkin watched in horror as his toothbrush flew past his ear, disappearing into the blackness of the plughole! A moment later the shampoo got sucked into the bath and *FLUP!*

It disappeared as well. Soon everything was flying into the bath and disappearing down the plughole! Soap, towels, sponges, toilet rolls, everything got sucked in. Even the contents of the cupboards were vacuumed down the plughole!

"HELP!" yelled Dinkin, as he felt himself being pulled towards the bath! He gripped the sink as tightly as he could, but the force was too great – within seconds his legs were lifted into the air!

As his fingers started to slip, Dinkin closed his eyes, and said (as quickly as he could):

"Frightening Things, Frightening Things,
Creep from the gloom,
Crawl from the shadows and into my room,
Frightening Things, Frightening Things,
Come to my aid,
Save me from danger and—"

Dinkin felt his fingers slip! He was lifted into the air, and lost his grip! His arms flailed wildly for something to grab. He saw ceiling, then floor, then blackness as he was sucked down the plughole!

"YaaaHHHHHHaaaHHHHHHaaaHHHaaaHHHHHHHH..."

(this is where Dinkin took a breath)

"YaaaHHHHHHHaaaHHHHHHaaaHHHaaaHHHHHHH..."

he screamed as he hurtled down a large, winding pipe. Down and round and up and even occasionally looping-the-loop. Try as he might, Dinkin couldn't stop. He just kept sliding, every now and again overtaking a toothbrush or loofah.

Finally, when he thought he couldn't fall (or scream) any more...

POP!
SPOOOOSH!

...he landed in a pool of water! Dinkin checked to see he hadn't lost anything important. He certainly looked a sorry state, in soaking wet pyjamas and his ridiculously wide, flat (and wet) hat-beard. It was then Dinkin realized he was surrounded. Several large shapes loomed over him. He rubbed the water out of his eyes and slowly looked up.

FISH-MEN!!

They were real! And there were *loads* of them! Wherever he looked, Dinkin could see giant, mutated fish creatures. They were *huge* and covered in big, shiny scales. They had round, black eyes and mouths full of sharp teeth, and they slid about on

thick, tail-like legs. The largest, most horrible-looking Fish-Man stepped forward. "Our fishy senses have not betrayed us – we finally have you!" said the Fish-Man. "Welcome to the kingdom of the Fish-Men! Welcome … to your doom!"

WELCOME ...
TO YOUR DOOM!

Probability of being welcomed to
your doom: 100%

"You're real..." whimpered Dinkin, as he shivered in the pool of grey water. He would have felt rather pleased with himself, if not for being paralyzed with fear.

"Of course we're real! I am Number One of the Fish-Men! And you ... are actually a lot shorter than I remember," said the Fish-Man. "No matter! Welcome ... to your doom!"

"You already said that..." said another Fish-Man.

"Did I? Oh, sorry... Now where was I? Oh yes – behold our underground kingdom!"

Dinkin looked around. There was a whole world under his house! He was in a huge cavern dug out of the sewers. It was dark, dank and naturally smelled of fish.

"After we escaped from Secret Sector Omega 3, we retreated here to the sewers, to plot our revenge!" And with that, all the Fish-Men raised their fins. Sure enough, on the end of each fin was an actual hand. But while they still had their thumbs, their fingers were missing.

"I didn't mean to eat your fingers! I was distracted! My dad grew a moustache!" screamed Dinkin, horrified beyond all reason.

"Silence! We will not listen to your lies. Look above you," instructed Number One.

Dinkin looked up. A thousand-and-one coiled pipes stretched above him, spreading out like a giant, metal spider's web. Each pipe emerged from the top of the cavern and led downwards, eventually connecting to a single pipe above the water pool.

"What ... what is it?" asked Dinkin, who was both curious and terrified at the same time.

"We call them ... the Pipes of Revenge!" said Number One, dramatically.

"I thought we were calling them the Channels of Justice," said another Fish-Man.

"I voted for the Tunnels of Retribution," said another.

"They're the Pipes of Revenge, end of story!" shouted Number One, then noticed Dinkin shivering with confused terror. "Where did I get to ... oh, yes. Each of these pipes leads to a bath in a human house," said Number One.

When we sense that our fingers have been eaten, we suck the offending human down the plughole! Then we welcome them ... to their doom!"

"You already said doom," said another Fish-Man.

"Did I? I hate delivering these big speeches, I always forget where I am ... the point is we've been waiting down here for a chance to capture you. Did you know we could sense your every move with our uncanny fishy senses? We were bound to get you in the end! The trouble was we still haven't managed to build our pipes all the way to your house on Levinson Drive yet. And the factory's even worse. What is it, ten miles away? It takes us for ever to connect these pipes... I mean, hello! No fingers! But then you did us the enormous favour of moving house ... right on top of our secret lair!"

"Wh-what? I didn't m-move house," said Dinkin, shivering with fear and cold.

"Lies will not save you! Welcome ... to your doom!"

"YOU ALREADY SAID DOOM!" cried the Fish-Men.

"I give up! Does someone else want to deliver the big speeches? Well? Number Three? Number Twenty-seven?" said Number One. He started to argue with the other Fish-Men, completely forgetting about Dinkin.

Dinkin looked around for any sign of the Frightening Things, but they were nowhere to be seen. He quickly decided on two possible courses of action: a) stay and be turned into fish food, or b) make a run for it. B) sounded slightly better, if just as terrifying as a). There was no obvious escape route – just pipes as far as the eye could see. He leaped to his feet and clambered up one as fast as he could.

"He's getting away!" screamed one of the Fish-Men.

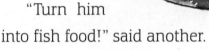

"Turn him into fish food!" said another.

"Make him pay!"

"Pull his beard!"

The Fish-Men tried to climb the pipe, but without fingers it was quite tricky. And the further Dinkin got, the steeper the climb became. Before long, he was stranded.

"Shake him off!" cried Number One. The Fish-Men began banging the pipe with their fingerless fists. *TUNG! TUNG! TUNG!* Dinkin tried to hold on, but it was no use – he felt his fingers slip...

FRIGHTENING THINGS TO THE RESCUE!

Chances of the Frightening Things
trying to rescue Dinkin: 99.4%
Chances of Edgar losing
his head: 99.5%
Chances of rescue
going smoothly: 0.0006%

"Dinkin, hang on!" came a cry. From out of the bottom of the pipe, the Frightening Things appeared! Arthur had turned them all ghostly. He was carrying Herbert, who in turn held Edgar by the feet. Edgar stretched out his bony arms as Dinkin fell.

"Reach out!" said Edgar, grabbing Dinkin's hand, and turning him ghostly too! The Fish-Men swiped angrily at him but their fingerless hands just passed straight through.

"You came!" cried Dinkin. "What took you so long? I was nearly fish food!"

"Sorry, Dinkin, it took us ages to work out where you'd gone! It's not every day someone disappears down the plug—" began Edgar, then did a double take. "Um, if you don't mind me asking, why are you wearing that ridiculously wide, flat hat and white beard?"

"It's a long story..." said Dinkin. "Now get us out of here!"

"Hang on tight, everyone! We have to keep the connection to all stay ghostly!" said Arthur.

"Stop them!" cried Number One. The Fish-Men raced after them, leaping into the air and gnashing their jaws. The Frightening Things (and Dinkin) all screamed in unison as they dodged and weaved through the army of scaly sea-beasts.

"They can't do anything to us while we're

ghostly. Back up the pipe! Get us out of here!" said Dinkin.

Arthur flew everyone through the Fish-Men, who tried desperately to bite or hit them, but only succeeded in biting or hitting each other. Finally, they arced upwards towards the pipe.

"We're nearly there! Everyone hang on!" said Dinkin. They were just about to reach the pipe when:

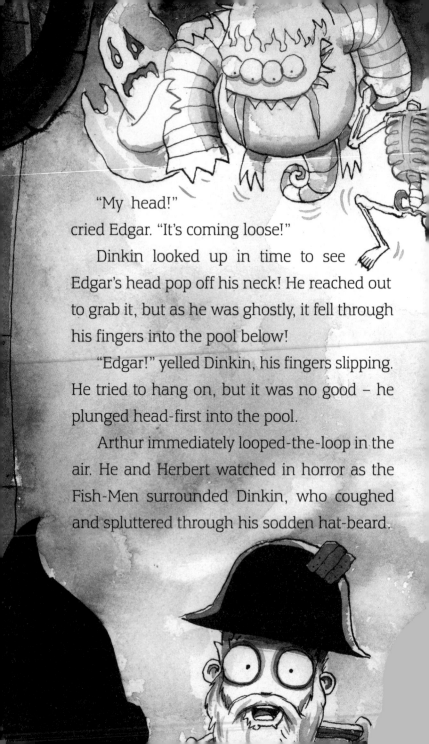

"My head!" cried Edgar. "It's coming loose!"

Dinkin looked up in time to see Edgar's head pop off his neck! He reached out to grab it, but as he was ghostly, it fell through his fingers into the pool below!

"Edgar!" yelled Dinkin, his fingers slipping. He tried to hang on, but it was no good – he plunged head-first into the pool.

Arthur immediately looped-the-loop in the air. He and Herbert watched in horror as the Fish-Men surrounded Dinkin, who coughed and spluttered through his sodden hat-beard.

"Fish-Men, our wait is over! At last we will have revenge on the evil mastermind who took our fingers! Death ... to Admiral Anchor!"

"*Please* don't eat me!" screamed Dinkin, cradling Edgar's head in his hands. "I didn't mean to eat your fingers, I was just ... wait! Did you say *Admiral Anchor?*"

"Yes, *you*, Admiral Anchor, the evil mastermind!" said Number One. "You who turned us from happy, stupid fish into giants with fingers, too hideous to walk the earth, and too big to fit into a fishtank."

"But I'm not Admiral Anchor!" said Dinkin.

"He's really not!" said Edgar's head.

"It's true!" shouted Herbert and Arthur together.

"Rubbish! There's no mistaking Admiral Anchor! Especially not with that ridiculously wide, flat hat and big white beard! We'd know you anywhere!" said Number One. Dinkin clutched at his hat – he'd completely forgotten he was wearing it.

"But it's true!" cried Dinkin, tearing off the hat-beard and throwing it into the pool. "I'm Dinkin Dings! Please don't turn me into fish food!"

The Fish-Men recoiled in horror, and a loud gasp echoed through the cavern.

"What is this trickery? You're not Admiral Anchor! You're just a little boy!" cried Number One.

"Y-yes, I'm D-Dinkin Dings..." said Dinkin, cowering in the pool. "But ... Admiral Anchor isn't Admiral Anchor either. He's an actor, called Simon. He gave me the hat-beard..."

"What rubbish..." laughed Number One. "I mean, if you're not Admiral Anchor, and Admiral Anchor isn't Admiral Anchor, then who's the evil mastermind?" asked Number One.

"Why, I am, of course!" came the cry from inside the pipe!

POP!
SPOOOOSH!

Dinkin leaped out of the way as someone fell out of the pipe and landed in the pool! As he dragged himself to his feet, Dinkin could just make out a blue-and-white striped T-shirt and small, white hat.

"Pip Ahoy!"

AHOY LOT OF TROUBLE

Chances of the truth being
revealed in a big speech: 88.8%
Chances of Fish-Men actually
having "fishy senses": 2.4%
Chances of evil mastermind
letting Dinkin go home: 0.003%

"*You* were the evil mastermind all along!" said Dinkin.

"Don't sound so surprised – that squealing buffoon you met in the factory is just my disguise, so that no one suspects me!" said Pip Ahoy, sounding far more deep-voiced and villainous than he did before. "Of *course* I'm the real mastermind! Who else could have created the Fish-Men? Who else could have made their fingers so tasty? Such a scheme requires a true *genius* – me, Pip Ahoy, the greatest mastermind the world has ever known!"

"Impossible!" cried Number One. "Admiral Anchor must be the evil mastermind – we felt it with our fishy senses!"

Pip Ahoy started to giggle. "I'm sorry, but 'fishy senses'?! That's the most ridiculous thing I've ever heard! What did you think, that you were *psychic?* You're a Fish-Man! Do you know many psychic fish?"

"Actually, I did think that bit sounded a bit far-fetched," whispered Dinkin.

"Silence! How dare you cast doubt on our fishy senses! How else do you explain our ability to locate Admiral Anchor?" That just made Pip Ahoy laugh even more!

"You dopes! There is no Admiral Anchor! Let me explain: when you escaped from Secret Sector Omega 3, I knew you'd want revenge on the mastermind who created you! I certainly didn't want you finding out it was me, so I hired an actor to play Admiral Anchor, the man behind 'Something Fishy' fish fingers!" Pip fished the hat-beard out of the water. "Oh, and to make sure you went after him instead of me, I fitted his hat-beard with a hypersonic transmitter signal that constantly beamed the Admiral's location directly into your brain ... your so-called 'fishy sense' was just my transmitter messing with your brainwaves! Then I used that same transmitter to find out where you've been hiding – once I realized the hat-beard had gone underground, I tracked the signal here ... and guess what? Here you all are! All ready for me to destroy you!"

"See? Now *that's* how you deliver a big speech," said a Fish-Man.

"Shut up! I've had enough of this! You took our fingers! You must pay!" said Number One, as he began to advance on Pip. "Fish-Men, get him!"

"Not so fast!" said Pip, whipping out an impressive, secret weapon-type ray gun from behind his back. Had Dinkin not been filled with unimaginable dread, he might have felt a bit of invention-related jealousy. "Do you think I wouldn't come prepared? This is my patented Anti-Fish-Men Dis-Fish-tegrator™ gun! It can disintegrate twenty Fish-Men at the touch of a button!"

"Um ... seeing as this isn't really anything to do with us, can we go home, please?" whimpered a petrified Dinkin, picking up Edgar's head again.

"Ah yes, the boy from the factory! How close you got to discovering Secret Sector Omega 3," said Pip with a sneer.

"What? No! I was just looking for the toilet!" cried a horrified Dinkin.

"A likely story!" cackled Pip. "And once I've finished with the Fish-Men it'll be your turn ... and who knows what horrible things my Dis-Fish-tegrator™ will do to you?"

"AAAA-A-A-AAAAAH!" squealed Dinkin and the Frightening Things. Pip charged the Dis-Fish-tegrator™ and took aim... "Pathetic Fish-Men, who will save you now?"

Dinkin looked around for someone to rescue them, but no one appeared. Which meant that once Pip had Dis-Fish-tegrated the Fish-Men, he and the Frightening Things were next. He looked down at Edgar's head...

"I hope you're not thinking of doing something silly..." whispered Edgar, but it was too late. Dinkin lifted it up, took aim, and threw it as hard as he could!

TWOINK!

Edgar's head hit Pip in the head! He fell backwards, firing the Dis-Fish-tegrator™ into the air.

ZWA-ZOOOOORK! A bolt of electric blue energy shot into the cavern. It bounced *PYEW!* off one of the pipes, then *PYEW!* off another, then *PYEW! PYEW! PYEW! PYEW!* ... until it streaked back towards Pip!

"AAAAHHAAaaH!" he screamed, holding the Dis-Fish-tegrator™ in front of his face.

SPWA-KOOOOM!

The Dis-Fish-tegrator™ exploded in a shower of sparks and smoke!

"I say, Dinkin, that's using your head," said Edgar's head.

"No, you can't defeat me! The evil mastermind never gets defeated!" yelled Pip Ahoy, as the Fish-Men surrounded him. "Stupid Fish-Men! I am your master! Obey me! Ow!" cried Pip.

"Oh no ... now you will obey us!" said Number One. "In fact, until we get our fingers back, we're going to make you do all the jobs we can't – cooking, cleaning scratching ourselves in hard-to-reach places..."

"NOOOOOOOO!" screamed Pip. As Dinkin watched the Fish-Men drag the evil mastermind away, he suddenly felt rather pleased with himself.

"Come on, let's get out of here while we have a chance..." he said, handing Edgar his head.

"Not so fast," growled Number One. "You may have saved us from the evil mastermind, but there's still the whole revenge-on-all-who-ate-our-fingers deal. Exactly how many of our fingers *did* you eat?"

"Well, uh, only one or two ... maybe three," whimpered Dinkin, as he and the Frightening Things backed away in terror. Number One lumbered towards them, his fingerless hands reaching out.

"Fingerless..." muttered Dinkin, a desperate, ridiculous thought occurring to him.

Number One paused for a second in mid-lunge. "Well, there's no need to rub it in," he said, suddenly feeling rather self-conscious about his hands.

"Give me ten minutes! If you don't eat me for ten minutes, I'll give you a reason not to!" said Dinkin in his most pleading tone.

"What are you planning, Dinkin?" whispered Edgar.

"I'll tell you in ten minutes," whimpered Dinkin. "If we're still here..."

THE DEAL

Number of fish fingers: 8
Number of deals struck: 1

Dinkin whispered something to Arthur, who immediately flew back up into the pipes and disappeared. For the next nine minutes and thirty-two seconds, Dinkin, Herbert and Edgar huddled together in fear, as the Fish-Men loomed over them.

"Time's up," said Number One, baring his teeth.

"Dinkin, catch!" said Arthur as he flew out of the pipe. He swooped over the Fish-Men and dropped a small, rectangular box into Dinkin's hands. It was blue and had a cartoon of an old man on it with a white beard and a ridiculously wide, flat hat. On it was written:

"SOMETHING FISHY" FISH FINGERS
OUR SECRET RECIPE MAKES THESE THE FISHIEST FISH FINGERS YOU'LL FIND!

The Fish-Men froze. They stared at the box, transfixed. They were like moths to a fishy flame.

"Where ... where did you get those...?" whispered Number One.

"From the freezer in our kitchen. If you'll agree not to eat me for a few more seconds, I'd like to try something," said Dinkin. He opened the fish finger packet and took out four fish fingers. Then he placed them, one by one, on the end of Number One's right hand. As he placed the fourth finger, he said,

"There you go. Fish fingers."

Number One stared at his hand, and then wiggled his breadcrumb-covered digits. They worked perfectly!

"I have *fingers*!" said Number One, a salty tear rolling down his cheek.

"And there's plenty more where that came from! My mum can get all the fish fingers you need! Enough for everyone!" said Dinkin.

"We could *all* have fingers? Oh, to be able to count, and point, and do 'rabbit ears' behind people's heads..." said Number One. He began to drift off into a haze of happy memories, before remembering where he was. "Ahem! And I suppose you expect me to spare your life in return?" he snarled.

"Actually, I was sort of thinking you wouldn't need to do the 'revenge on all those who ate our fingers' thing at all," said Dinkin, quietly. "I mean, if that's OK with you."

Number One wiggled his new fingers again and grinned. "Agreed! We shall call off our attack on humankind, and you shall get us fish fingers! But if you fail us, then you will be the first to be turned into fish food!"

"Deal..." whimpered Dinkin, wondering where he was going to get that many fish fingers from.

Dinkin and the Frightening Things didn't hang around any longer than they had to – as soon as the Fish-Men let them go, they flew back up through the pipe. By the time they reached the bathroom, Dinkin's mother was knocking on the door.

"Are you OK in there, Dinkin? I heard a noise, and you've been a very long time..."

"I think we'd best be off," said Edgar. "There's no point in us all getting in trouble."

"I suppose not," said Dinkin. Arthur flew the Frightening Things through the bathroom wall into Dinkin's bedroom.

Dinkin looked around. The bathroom was devastated, and completely empty. Almost everything had been sucked down the plughole (which now, of course, looked perfectly normal). He sighed as his mum opened the door.

"Oh my – Dinkin! What have you done? It looks like there's been a tornado in here!" she screamed. "And where are all our *things*?"

Dinkin just shrugged and said, "You know how you said that things are really rather normal? Well, sometimes, they're really, really not."

A REALLY LONG STORY

Temperature: 13°C
Outlook: cloudy, light rain, with
a good chance of Fish-Men

The next morning, at breakfast, Dinkin chewed sluggishly on a piece of toast.

"I still don't understand what you did with everything in the bathroom," said Mrs Dings as she sipped a cup of coffee. "I'm not sure your father will ever forgive you for losing his favourite loofah."

"You wouldn't believe me if I told you," sighed Dinkin.

"Well, you're not having any more pocket money until you've paid for everything you lost," said his mum.

"But it wasn't..." began Dinkin, then decided it was a really long story, and she wouldn't believe it anyway. He just shook his head and said, "Never mind."

"Well, I'm off to the supermarket – is there anything you'd like me to pick up for dinner?" said Mrs Dings.

Just then the kitchen sink started to shake. It made the tap judder and water bubbled up from the plughole. Dinkin froze, his eyes wide with terror.

"Oh, don't worry, that pipe's always getting blocked," said Mrs Dings. "So, is there anything you'd especially like?"

"Fish fingers," said Dinkin, shaking. "*Lots* of fish fingers."